CONGRESS PARK SCHOOL
District 102
Brookfield, Il.

THE TRUE
STORY OF
Christmas

ANNE FINE

DELACORTE PRESS

Published by
Delacorte Press
an imprint of
Random House Children's Books
a division of Random House, Inc.
New York

Visit us on the Web! www.randomhouse.com/kids
Educators and librarians, for a variety of teaching tools, visit us at www.randomhouse.com/teachers

Library of Congress Cataloging-in-Publication Data
Fine, Anne.
The true story of Christmas / Anne Fine.
p.   cm.
Summary: A Christmas quiz brings out some hidden truths for the Mountfield family.
ISBN 0-385-73130-2 (trade) — ISBN 0-385-90156-9 (GLB)
[1. Christmas—Fiction. 2. Family life—Fiction. 3. Humorous stories.] I. Title.
PZ7.F495673Tr 2003
[Fic]—dc21
2003005166

Printed in the United States of America

September 2003

10 9 8 7 6 5 4 3 2 1

BVG

THE MOUNTFIELD CHRISTMAS TREE

DRAWN BY RALPH MOUNTFIELD

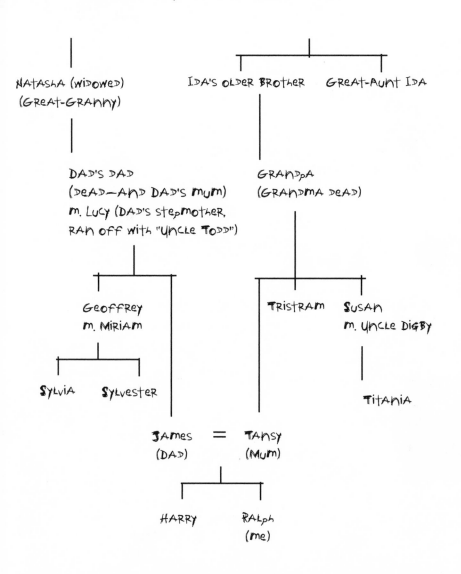

NATASHA (WIDOWED)
(GREAT-GRANNY)

IDA'S OLDER BROTHER   GREAT-AUNT IDA

DAD'S DAD
(DEAD—AND DAD'S mum)
m. LUCY (DAD'S stepmother,
RAN OFF WITH "UNCLE TODD")

GRANDPA
(GRANDMA DEAD)

Geoffrey
m. MIRIAM

TRISTRAM   SUSAN
                m. UNCLE DIGBY

SYLVIA   SYLVESTER

                              TITANIA

JAMES   =   TANSY
(DAD)   (MUM)

HARRY   RALPH
             (me)

LOOKING FORWARD
TO CHRISTMAS?

BE WARNED!

MY SIDE OF THE STORY

Perhaps you'd care to hear my side of the story? Here am I, Ralph William Mountfield, banished to my bedroom on Christmas Day, with no one even giving me a chance to explain. But it was all Titania's fault, really. Everyone said we were just putting on an act when we stood, hands spread, mouths open, insisting there was nothing we could have done.

"Acting all injured," said Aunt Miriam.

"If you put both of them in a bag and punched it, whichever one you hit would deserve it," said Great-granny.

But everyone knows I can't act. My brother, Harry, can. He played the Slough of Despond—that means bog of despair—when our school put on *Pilgrim's Progress,* and it's not easy, acting a mud swamp. But all I've ever been allowed to be is one of the oysters in "The Walrus and the Carpenter" in this year's Christmas show. (And even then, everyone complained that I looked far too happy while I was being eaten.)

So I couldn't have been putting it on. But even if I were, I would have been about the only person in the house who wasn't wearing a false face and saying things they didn't mean.

Titania's Christmas Quiz proved that.

TITANIA

Neither Harry nor I can stand Titania. (No one can, actually.) Her mum is our mum's sister, so we are cousins, and ever since she was born she's come to stay twice a year. She wasn't too bad when she was a baby. Even as a toddler she wasn't all that much trouble, lying for hours in her little barred travel bed, talking to her fingers. (I even caught her singing to the wallpaper once—a song called "Mucking About in the Garden.")

We had a good game with her too. You see, for years, she couldn't say her *r*s properly, so Harry and I quite enjoyed trailing her round the house, teasing her till she told us we were "weally wery wubbish!"

But then Aunt Susan decided that Titania was "gifted." (Everyone in our family thought she was just a dreadful

5

know-all, but there you are, that's parents for you.) And after that, Titania became intolerable. We had to sit quietly about a million times (without even being allowed to snigger) while she did her "I'm a Little Teapot" performance. Then she took to saying that she could see fairies at the bottom of the garden, and wearing frocks so stupid and frilly that once, when she lost her pretend diamond necklace, it must have been half an hour before it even managed to work its way far enough down to get found again in her knickers.

I used to have to hold her hand all the way to the shop when she wanted to buy her "fairy dust" (pink sherbet). It was embarrassing. I used to tell everyone she was off to a fancy-dress party. Harry wouldn't hold her hand at all. If it was his turn to take her, he'd simply bribe me into doing it.

"What, only fifty pence?" I'd complain.

"It's not much, is it?" he'd admit. "But it looks quite a lot, sitting next to nothing."

So I'd agree to go.

Harry gets what he wants a lot more often than I do. He's a year older than I am and Mum's favorite. (Mum says she doesn't have a favorite, but I wasn't born yesterday.)

THE REST OF THE FAMILY

The easiest way of introducing you to everyone else is to tell you three of the things I heard them saying over the last two days.

MUM:

"Oh, Ralph. Be an angel and see if the coast is clear all the way to the bathroom."

"Ralph, darling, would you just carry this toast through for me?"

"Ralph, poppet. Be a sweetie, and rush up and fetch Daddy his aspirins."

DAD:

"I regret, Ralph, that, due to the demands of this

stupid oversized turkey, this area of the kitchen is temporarily closed to idle traffic such as yourself."

"My head feels like a lump of boiled owl."

"Does anyone else think this toast tastes like buttered Brillo pads?"

UNCLE TRISTRAM
(he's my mum's brother, and he's thirty-one):

"Hi, Ralph. I was just enjoying myself throwing spuds at this cat through the window."

"Shhh! Don't distract me. I'm listing the ten things I hate most about Great-granny."

"I found this child abandoned in the bath. It's wrinkled as a prune. Does anyone want it?"

GREAT-GRANNY:

"If I had my own teeth, I'd bite you."

"By the time I was your age, I had read Milton."

"Try not to act sillier than you look."

GREAT-AUNT IDA:

"I'd love to help you in the kitchen, Tansy, but what with my very weak wrist . . ."

"I'd offer to lay the dining room table for lunch for

you, Tansy, but my poor dear wrist would simply shriek, 'No!'"

"Help wash up? Oh, impossible! My wrist bone is as brittle as crispbread. Can't you find someone else?"

GRANDPA

(this will be easier to follow if I explain that Grandpa mostly walks round with his toolbox, singing to our dog, Bruno, and explaining to him how he plans to fix things):

"I can't go hunting with you, Jake,
'Cause I'm out chasin' wimmin . . ."

"As you'll see, Bruno, someone has used quite the wrong size of screw here, and that has contributed appreciably to the problem."

"Roses round the door,
Babies on the floor,
Happy vall-eee, happy vall-ee—
And yoo-oooo."

There are a few more people in the house, but that's enough to get you started.

CHRISTMAS EVE

WRITING LETTERS TO SANTA

O n Christmas Eve morning, everyone arrived in their separate clumps, and there was all the usual fuss about bagging the best beds and warmest rooms. Great-granny wanted windows facing south. ("So she can quarrel with the moon all night," Dad suggested.)

Then Great-aunt Ida had to tell us all about her "twisted wrist." ("That makes a change," said Mum. "Usually it's a sprained ankle so she can park in the comfiest chair and not move for six days.")

After that, Titania had one of her "sensitive" fits, saying she wouldn't be able to sleep in the room she'd been given because "the wall has got stains in the shapes of ugly faces."

"You ought to feel more at home, then," Harry said.

He got sent to his room for that. So then, of course, I was the one who had to swap beds with Titania. (And *still* Mum claims Harry isn't her favorite.)

Then Aunt Susan dragged everyone out for a nature walk. (Harry got out of it by pretending he hadn't heard Mum say he could come down again.) There is a limit to how exciting anyone can make the life history of a holly berry sound, so I wasn't really listening when she went on to mistletoe.

As soon as we'd got home again, Titania decided the next thing she wanted to do was write a letter to Santa. This is the sort of soppy idea that makes Aunt Susan clap her hands and say Titania is "so uncynical." (Dad calls it "daft for her age.")

"Oh, really. Not now," Mum said. "I'm about to set the table."

But Aunt Susan gave her a look, and Mum gave up and agreed she could leave setting the table till later.

"Won't the boys join Titania?" asked Aunt Susan.

Harry snorted and left the room. I made to follow but Mum collared me. "You'll stay, Ralph, won't you? Just to keep Titania company?"

"What, sit and write a betsy-wetsy letter to Santa? Are you joking?"

"Shhh!" Mum reproved me. "Be polite." (Which means "Don't scrap with me in front of visitors.")

Defeated, I slumped at the table. Aunt Susan gave me a few sheets of plain paper. Titania rushed upstairs to fetch her own out of her suitcase. (It was smelly and pink and sprinkled with glitter.)

I wrote:

DEAR SANTA,

FOR CHRISTMAS, I WOULD LIKE A SKUNK, A REAL DEAD HUMAN SKULL, A VESPA PX125, A MOTORIZED GLITTER BALL, A KING OF THE FROGS POSTER, A RIDE IN A HOT-AIR BALLOON—

"Mummy!" called Titania. "Ralph's being horribly, horribly greedy!"

—A GAME BOY ADVANCE, A FLIGHT IN A TIGER MOTH, A SIDE OF SMOKED SALMON, A PAIR OF ROCKER GTS HEADPHONES, AND A DAY WHITE-WATER RAFTING DOWN THE COLORADO RIVER.

Titania wrote:

DEAR, DEAR, LOVELY, SWEET MR. SANTA—

"Crawler!" I accused her.

"Mummy!" she called. "Mum-mee! Ralph is calling me names!"

"Oh, get on with it," I told her.

She got on with it.

—AND ALL YOUR BEAUTIFUL PRANCING REINDEER,
I HOPE YOU HAVE HAD A SIMPLY LOVELY AND RESTFUL
YEAR AND ARE NOW READY FOR CHRISTMAS. IF YOU
THINK I'VE BEEN GOOD ENOUGH—

I stuck my finger in my mouth and made the throw-up sign.

—THEN WHAT I'D LOVEY, LOVEY, DOVE, LOVE FOR
CHRISTMAS IS AN A-DORA-BLE LITTLE MISS DORA
DOLLY, A MILKMAID OUTFIT, AND, IF YOU REALLY WANT
TO SPOIL ME, ONE OF THOSE LITTLE KITTEN KEY
RINGS YOU CAN GET AT THE CO-OP.
OH, THANK YOU, THANK YOU, THANK YOU.

LOVE AND KISSES,
TITANIA

XXXXXXXXXXXXXXX
P.S. PLEEEEEEE-EEEEEEEEEASE!

I wrote my own P.S.

P.S. FORGET JUST ONE TINY THING, SANTA, AND YOU'LL
BE PICKING YOUR TEETH UP WITH A BROKEN ARM.

"We have to post them to the North Pole now," Titania
told me. "So we have to design our own pretty little
Toytown stamps."

She wheedled at Mum until she knocked off peeling
her potato mountain and found some felt pens. Then
Titania leaned over the table, humming one of her "fairy
songs," and drew an elf on a little hill waving as a team of
reindeer flew over his head through a sprinkle of multi-
colored glitter.

"Do you know what that is?" she asked me, pointing to
the glistening shower.

I took a guess. "Radioactive anthrax spores?"

"It's magic stardust."

She leaned over to look at my stamp—a pretty pass-
able Slasher Santa storming out of a chimney with all his
blades flashing.

"That's not very nice," she said. "If you send Santa
that, he might not bring you all the things you asked for."

"Well, try and astonish me some other way," I muttered.

UNCLE TRISTRAM'S BRICKS

I did a fast bunk. On the way upstairs, I bumped into Uncle Tristram, carrying two halves of a brick.

"What are those for?" I asked.

He turned all furtive. "Mind your own business."

He hid the bricks behind his back when Dad came out of the bathroom, warbling a song about turning armpits into charmpits.

"Skulking away up here, are you, James?" Uncle Tristram asked Dad sourly. "Don't you think it's time you got dressed again and went down to face the enemy?"

(He meant Great-granny.)

Dad knotted the towel more tightly round his waist. "I think I can safely claim I offered my share of seasonal pleasantries over her early-morning tea tray. But

17

perhaps you, Tristram, as someone whose feet are regularly planted firmly and squarely under our dining table, could go down and do a stint."

Uncle Tristram fought back. "I didn't invite her. And she's more your relation than mine."

As he spoke, he was backing toward the box room he's been told to park in until Great-aunty Ida goes back in her Home. He was still trying to keep his two halves of brick hidden.

"And I *have* done my bit for the morning," he added. "You may have been a grand success with your tea tray, but ever since then she's been working herself into a froth about the catering."

"It isn't 'catering,' " my father said. "It is my poor wife, Tansy, cooking for a whole pack of picky and ungrateful people."

I piped up. "I'm not ungrateful."

Dad turned on me. "Do you eat fried tomatoes?"

"Not if they still have skins on," I admitted.

"Mushrooms?"

"Only if they're raw."

He played his trump card. "And do you eat coconut, even in curries where the amounts are so infinitesimal that only a forensic pathologist would really be expected to work out they are there?"

I hung my head. "No."

"So it could be fairly argued you fall under the heading 'picky.' "

"Don't bark at Ralph," Uncle Tristram said. "Just be a man, take your turn and go down and do your next shift."

Dad turned all virtuous. "I think I can safely claim I've done my fair share this morning. I had quite a struggle earlier, helping her out of her overcoat."

"She says that's because she was trying to put it on."

Dad looked rather hopeful. "Why? Was she planning to go out?"

"How should I know? Perhaps she was getting into the Christmas spirit and going off to look for some firstborns to slaughter."

"But where is she now?"

"Back in the living room, picking a row with the rugs for trying to trip her." He sighed. "I only hope, when I'm that age, somebody gives me an injection."

I had another go at joining in their conversation. "Harry says," I told them, "that, if you get close enough to her, you can smell embalming fluid."

Both of them turned on me.

"*You* go!" they chorused. "You go down there and have a turn looking after Great-granny."

TRYING TO GET OUT OF IT

First, I tried to get out of it. I went into the kitchen to find Mum.

"Dad says I have to go and talk to Great-granny. I don't have to, do I? Say I don't have to!"

"Ralph, sweetheart, don't you think it would be nice to get to know her just a little bit better?"

"No. I think I know her quite well enough, thanks."

"You might *enjoy* talking to her."

I let that one pass. After a moment Mum went red in the face and said, "Well, *she* might enjoy it."

"Yes," I said. "I expect she also enjoys pulling the wings off flies and eating tin tacks."

"Ralph," said Mum. "Do as your father tells you. Go and be civil to Great-granny."

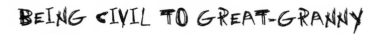

BEING CIVIL TO GREAT-GRANNY

I went in. Great-aunt Ida was chuntering on to the air about whether or not it was Wednesday, and Great-granny was back to thrashing around inside her moth-eaten fur coat.

"Are you getting in or out?" I asked before stepping forward to help her.

She looked at me as if I had no brain. "Out, of course."

"Just checking," I said hastily.

She got a bit of a nasty look in her eye then. So, as I was holding her sleeve for her, I tried to think of something really civil to say. The most polite person I know is Dad's stepmother, Aunt Lucy. (As soon as she heard that Great-granny was coming again, she said she was going to Madeira for Christmas.)

21

Aunt Lucy would probably have struck up a conversation with me by saying something like "Are you getting excited about Christmas, dear?" But that didn't sound quite right for Great-granny. Especially the "dear" bit. So in the end I just said the first thing that popped into my head.

"Would you like me to tell you the story of *The Swiss Family Robinson*?"

"No, thank you," she said tartly.

"*Treasure Island?*" I offered.

She looked at me as if I were a grease spot on the carpet.

"*The Island of Adventure?*"

She turned toward Great-aunt Ida, as if even a conversation about whether or not it was Wednesday might be better than this. Realizing things weren't going well, I tried what I'd heard all the hairdressers asking people when I'd been waiting for Mum in the salon on Saturday.

"So. All ready for Christmas, then?"

Great-granny said darkly, "Don't get your hopes up. I shall be keeping a very tight grip on *my* purse."

So I gave up and started to tell the two of them a joke.

"There's this bar in the Wild West with no one inside except the barman. In comes this man and he orders a drink and says, 'So, why's the place empty?' and the barman says, 'Oh, everyone's out at the hanging.' So the man asks, 'Who's being hanged?' and the barman says, 'Brown Paper Pete.' "

Just at this moment the door flew open and in pranced Titania with a homemade glitter crown in her hair and wearing red ballet shoes. Acting as if I wasn't even on the planet, she said to Great-aunt Ida and Great-granny, "Would you like to hear me sing 'Lavender's Blue, Dilly, Dilly'?"

Great-granny gave her a bit of a brain-frying glare, but Great-aunt Ida broke off her chat to the air about whether or not it was Wednesday and said, "That would be lovely, dear. *Lovely.*"

Titania plucked at the handfuls of frills on the sides of her frock, did a soppy bobby curtsy and launched straight into it:

"Lavender's blue, dilly, dilly,
Lavender's green."

Stubbornly, I carried on. "And the man said, 'Brown Paper Pete? That's a very odd name, isn't it? Why is he called Brown Paper Pete?' "

Titania flounced past me, twirling and simpering.

"When I am king, dilly, dilly,
You'll be my queen."

" 'Well,' said the barman," I persisted. " 'The thing is

that Brown Paper Pete always wears a brown paper hat and a brown paper jacket.' "

Titania glowered at me as hard as you can when you're twirling and twittering.

"Call up your men, dilly, dilly,

Set them to work—"

" 'And brown paper trousers and brown paper socks,' " I pressed on determinedly.

"Some to the plow, dilly, dilly,

Some to the cart—"

" 'And he walks round in brown paper shoes.' "

"Some to make hay, dilly, dilly,

Some to cut corn—"

"And the man said, 'So what is he being hanged for, this Brown Paper Pete?' "

"While you and I, dilly, dilly—"

"And the barman said—"

"Keep ourselves warm."

" 'Rustling!' "

"I hope both of you get boils on your bottom," said Great-granny.

Mum poked her head round the door. "I do hope the children are entertaining you nicely. Just shoo them out if they're any problem."

I didn't wait to be shooed. I followed Mum out straightaway. "That was horrible. Horrible!"

Mum said reprovingly, "I hope you were civil to her, Ralph."

"I was perfectly civil to *her*," I said bitterly. "I just think she could have been a little more civil to *me*."

SNOWVILLE

Uncle Tristram was reading the paper in the kitchen with next door's Albert squatting on his feet, wrapped in a towel after being found in the bath again.

"Listen to this," Uncle Tristram was telling Mum. "There's this town called Snowville in Wyoming, and they found eight dismembered bodies in a barrel there."

"What's dismembered?" Albert piped up to ask him.

"Cut up in little bits," he said, grinning.

"Really, Tristram," my mum said. "Is this really suitable? Albert is only four."

"He's got to learn," said Tristram piously. "Anyhow, now the people of Snowville are selling all these jokey souvenirs in their gift shops. There's a fridge magnet with bits of a dismembered man in a barrel, that says, 'I've been to

Snowville.' And a mug shaped like a barrel with a spoon in the shape of a severed arm."

"What's severed?" Albert asked.

"Cut off," said Uncle Tristram. He saw Mum's look and added hastily, "He's got to *learn,* Tansy. And there's even a Snowville snow shaker, which has bits of body floating round instead of snow."

"What's a snow shaker?" Albert asked.

"Search me," said Uncle Tristram, and went back to his paper.

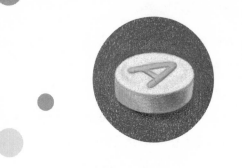

COUNTING

Mum said to Dad, "James, tell me how many we will be for lunch today."

Dad had a go at counting. "Well, there'll be you and me, and Harry and Ralph. Grandpa, of course, if he and Bruno ever get back from mending the front fence. And Digby and Susan and Titania—"

"Is Digby here?" Mum said. "I haven't seen him all morning. I thought he must have driven back to their house to fetch something they'd forgotten."

"He's upstairs, hiding," I informed her, adding bitterly, "Along with Harry."

"Hiding? Where?"

"In the airing cupboard."

"What are they doing?"

"Digby is reading last week's papers," I told her. "Harry is getting all his thank-you letters over and done with."

"But he doesn't even know what he's getting yet."

"He's leaving spaces for those bits."

"For heaven's sake!" said Mum. (She sounded really irritated.)

Dad carried on counting. "And Great-aunt Ida, and Great-granny, and Tristram here . . ." He stopped and peered over his fingers. "How many is that?"

"Eleven," I said.

"Ten," said Mum.

"I know I'd run out of fingers," Dad said. "So I think it must have been *at least* eleven."

"Is Albert staying?" I asked them.

"No," said Dad.

"If he wants to," Mum insisted.

Dad shook his finger at her. "All right. But don't come running to me again with complaints about having to feed a great army of ingrates."

"Hush!" Mum said.

"What's an ingrate?" asked Albert.

"Someone who doesn't say thank you to the cook properly after stuffing their face full," Uncle Tristram told him.

"Excuse *me*," Dad said to Tristram. "My lovely wife Tansy here is not 'the cook.' She is your gracious *hostess.*"

"Oh, bash me till you can sieve the bits," muttered Tristram.

"You stole that one off Great-granny," I accused him.

Mum broke it up, going toward the larder. "I'll cook for eleven, then, shall I?"

As she walked past the stove, the oven door crashed down. She slammed it up again.

"Now everyone's confused me," Dad complained. "I'm going to have to count again."

This time, he got to thirteen. "When are Miriam and Geoffrey and the twins coming?" (The twins are our other cousins.)

"Tomorrow," Mum said firmly. " 'Christmas Day only,' I told them. I couldn't have made it more plain. I explained there was no way on earth we could manage them before that."

"Not after last year," Dad said feelingly.

I thought they might be interested in something I knew and they didn't. "Uncle Todd said he'd had pleas-anter times fighting the Serbs," I informed them. "They're one of the reasons that he and Aunt Lucy have fled to Madeira."

"Please don't say 'fled to,' " Mum reproved me. "Just say 'chosen to spend Christmas in.' "

"All right," I said. "But it was fleeing, really. Uncle

Todd said that having the twins around last Christmas was like living in endless retakes of an X-rated horror film."

Dad shuddered at the memory. "Well, the garden shed's been rebuilt now. And the decorator did finally make some headway with the stains on the wall along the landing. I do still feel a little sore about that rug, because it was valuable. And the vet as good as admitted that the whole ugly business of their visit almost certainly hastened Thumper's untimely death, and did poor Bruno no good at all. I don't think he threw off that nervous tremble till Easter . . ."

Dad stared grimly into the past and then gave himself a little shake.

"But let's not spoil our pleasant Christmas Eve thinking about all that, shall we? Let's leave the worrying till they arrive tomorrow."

He counted again on his fingers. "Now I make it twelve."

Outside the house, there was the screech of tires on gravel and the slamming of car doors.

The back door flew open and in came the twins.

"Surprise!" yelled Sylvia.

"Surprise!" yelled Sylvester.

Then in came Miriam and Geoffrey. "We thought we'd come early to surprise you! You don't mind?"

"No, not at all," Mum said faintly. "It's quite all right. The more the merrier. Honestly."

"Sixteen," said Dad. Then inspiration struck. "That means we'll need another tub of ice cream. I'll whip down the shops."

But he was too late. Uncle Tristram had already got to the car keys.

GREAT-AUNT IDA'S (IMAGINARY) CHURCH VISIT

Over lunch, while Aunt Miriam was away chasing after Sylvia and Sylvester, who had taken the bread rolls and run from the table, Great-aunt Ida started to tell everyone about the church service she'd attended that morning.

"Nobody let her out, did they?" Dad asked anxiously around the table. "The Home said most particularly that we weren't supposed to let her out."

"Oh, yes, dear," said Great-aunt Ida. "I've been to morning communion at Wells Cathedral."

(Wells Cathedral is about seven hundred hours' drive from here, so Dad stopped worrying.)

"Did you enjoy it?" Mum said.

"It was a lovely service," Great-aunt Ida told her.

"I'm glad," said Mum. She turned to Great-granny. "More potatoes, Natasha?"

"No, thank you," said Great-granny. "They look a bit grubby."

"I took communion," said Great-aunt Ida proudly. "Even though the vicar was floating past the windows at the time."

"Much like those bread rolls," Uncle Tristram said.

We all looked out the window. Bread rolls were flying past.

"Yes!" Great-aunt Ida said. "It was like that. Except, of course, that the vicar floated past so much more slowly."

"Well, he would, wouldn't he?" said Uncle Tristram. "Holy communion being a much more serious matter than a mere bread-roll fight."

"We did have communion wafers, though," Great-aunt Ida assured him.

"Not too heavy for your poor wrist, I hope?" Dad said.

Mum signaled him to knock it off at once.

"And there was wine in the chalice," said Great-aunt Ida.

"That's nice," said Uncle Geoffrey. He looked hopefully toward my father. "I wouldn't mind a drop more wine my-self . . ."

Dad totally ignored him. He says if his sister's rich husband wants to drink himself stupid at every single meal over Christmas, he should go to the trouble of bringing a few bottles.

"And prawns, too," said Great-aunt Ida.

"What, in the chalice?" Mum asked, startled.

"Oh, yes, dear. The big sort. The ones you can buy at Tesco. I had three or four." She leaned across the table confidentially. "If you want my opinion, one could almost accuse the vicar of being *overly lavish.*"

"Unlike one or two people round here," Uncle Geoffrey muttered, pushing his empty wineglass forward one more time.

And this time, as before, my dad totally ignored him.

MEGATANTRUM

During the afternoon, Sylvia locked the cat in the greenhouse, where it scratched up Mum's *Tropaeolum canariense* seedlings. (Don't ask me what they are. But you could tell from the look on her face that you can't buy two for 99p down at any old Tesco.)

At teatime, Sylvester knocked the cake off the cake stand, and Sylvia knocked a leg off the papier-mâché owl I made for Mum when I was in nursery, so it fell off the mantelpiece and knocked its own ears off.

(Titania got all excited. "Sylvia's broken it! Look at her! She's broken Ralph's owl! She's really broken it!" so I had to pretend that I didn't care a button.)

After tea, Sylvia spilled Great-aunt Ida's coffee down

the arm of the cream sofa and didn't tell anyone, so by the time Mum noticed, it was too late to get the stain out.

And then, rushing about pretending to be a wolverine, Sylvester crashed into the telly.

Which went dead.

"If I had my own teeth, I'd bite you," said Great-granny.

Dad left the room. He said he didn't trust himself "not to strangle Sylvester on the spot." Uncle Tristram went down on his knees in front of the Christmas week schedules and wailed and wailed. "Oh, no! We're going to miss so much good stuff! Brilliant comedies! Terrific films! All the best shows! Disaster! Oh, it doesn't bear thinking about!"

Uncle Geoffrey looked baffled. "Surely there must be someone round here who would come out to fix it?"

"On Christmas Eve?" said Uncle Tristram. "Are you *mad*? That sort of service might happen where you live, Geoffrey, but not round here." He went back to the schedules. "Oh, no! Oh, no! And we're going to miss *Mars Attacks!* and *The Donny and Mopp Show*!"

Sylvester burst into tears. "Miss *The Donny and Mopp Show*? I can't! I can't! That's my total favorite!"

Uncle Tristram wailed more loudly. "Oh, no! This one is double length, and doubly special!"

Sylvester stamped on the rug. "I won't miss it! I won't miss it!"

"Now, now!" said Uncle Tristram, suddenly changing tack. "Mustn't be slaves to a machine, must we? Now, who would like a nice long session of that wonderful board game that teaches you geography instead?"

We all watched Sylvester have his megatantrum. Harry said he could hear his teeth gnashing. Great-granny said the way he chewed the fringe of the carpet brought Hitler to mind. Dad said he could hear it way out in the wood-shed. And in the end Uncle Geoffrey agreed to drive to their country cottage the other side of Worcester and pick up the telly his family kept in that house.

"Good job you didn't drink at lunch," said Uncle Tristram. (Mum told him afterward that that was *mean*.)

Sylvia and Sylvester went with Uncle Geoffrey, and, because they have a big posh car, Titania went too. As soon as they had vanished down the drive, Uncle Tristram took the missing little bit from the end of the aerial out of his pocket and twisted it back on the lead. Then he shoved the repaired end straight back into the telly and shoved in a tape to record *Mars Attacks!* while we all watched *The Donny and Mopp Show.*

Everyone enjoyed it. (Even Great-granny.)

Then Uncle Tristram and Dad and Harry and I played Mad Dogs round the house, while Mum went to bed with a book and "a headache." And by the time that lot got back, we'd all gone upstairs and the whole house was quiet.

CHRISTMAS MORNING

MY DEAR, SWEET CHILD

When I woke up on Christmas morning, there was an envelope pinned to the top of my stocking. I opened it first. Inside was a letter in Uncle Tristram's writing.

MY DEAR, SWEET CHILD,

THANK YOU FOR YOUR LOVEY, WOVEY, DOVEY LETTER ASKING FOR PRESENTS. BUT THERE IS A TEENSY-WEENSY PROBLEM. YOU SEE, THIS HOUSE YOU'RE STAYING IN FOR CHRISTMAS LIES IN A MAGIC DELL. BACK IN THE OLDEN DAYS, A VERY, VERY BAD FAIRY PUT A NASTY SPELL ON IT. YOU'LL GET YOUR PRESENTS ALL RIGHT. BUT IF YOU MAKE THE MISTAKE OF SINGING EVEN A SINGLE ONE OF YOUR PRETTY LITTLE

SONGS, OR DANCING EVEN A SINGLE ONE OF YOUR
PRETTY LITTLE DANCES, OR RECITING EVEN A SINGLE
ONE OF YOUR SWEET LITTLE POEMS, OR DROPPING SO
MUCH AS A SINGLE ONE OF YOUR ENCHANTING LITTLE
CURTSIES, EVERY ONE OF YOUR PRESENTS WILL HAVE
VANISHED BY MORNING.

SORRY ABOUT THIS. THAT'S JUST THE WAY IT IS.

HUGS AND KISSES,

SANTA

P.S. THE REINDEER SEND THEIR LOVE.
P.P.S. THIS IS A SECRET. TELL NO ONE.

I never sing or dance or recite poems or curtsy. I was
still wondering why Uncle Tristram had bothered when I
heard the scream.

TITANIA'S LETTER

T itania was running up and down the landing, tears spurting from her eyes. She had a letter in her hand.

"Look at it!" she was screeching. "Look at it!"

I took it from her. The letters sprawled over the page like the writing in a ransom note.

WRITE ANOTHER "DEAR SANTA . . ." LETTER LIKE THAT, KIDDO, AND I'LL BREAK IN YOUR BEDROOM AT DEAD OF NIGHT, SUCK YOUR BRAINS OUT OF YOUR HEAD THROUGH YOUR NOSE WITH A STRAW, AND STEAL ALL YOUR PRESENTS.

LOVE,
SANTA

P.S. IF YOU TELL YOUR MOTHER I WROTE THIS, I WILL
EAT YOUR DOG.

    Hearing the noise, Uncle Tristram came out of his box
room and took in the situation at a glance.

    "Whoops!" he said. "Bit of a mix-up there. Sorry about
that."

    Then he vanished behind the door and I didn't see him
again until breakfast.

IN MY STOCKING

Titania went off sobbing. I went back in my room and tipped out my stocking. Inside were a few crumbs from last year, some socks I needed anyway, a plastic rattlesnake, a book token, some jumping beans that didn't jump, a packet of Make Your Own Candy Floss, a chocolate shark, a widemouthed frog egg cup, some joke boxer shorts, a giant striped mint, an orange I could just as easily have taken out of the bowl, and a plastic potato that turned out to be a pencil sharpener.

And I couldn't help starting to think a bit.

What I was thinking was that, up to a point, Christmas is like a blown-up but not yet knotted balloon that's been let go by mistake. It goes *bla-a-a-a-a-a-a-are!* and then shrivels into not much. So all that time waiting, and looking forward, and hoping and expecting, is like the little puffs of air you use to fatten the balloon in the first place.

"What are you getting for Christmas?" (*Puff!*)

"I want a new bike. What do you want?" (*Puff!*)

"Will there be sausages as well as roast turkey?" (*Puff!*)

"Look what they're going to show on telly! Brilliant!" (*Puff!*)

You puff it up in your imagination, till the thought of it is all fat and shiny and perfect, like a balloon. But when you try to knot the neck of a balloon and your fingers slip, all the air rushes out, making a rude noise, and the balloon flies away from you, jiggling and juddering, and ends up lying on the floor looking all sad and shriveled, and as if it couldn't have been much in the first place.

Well, I'm beginning to think that Christmas is like that.

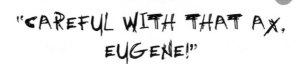

"CAREFUL WITH THAT AX, EUGENE!"

When I went down to the kitchen to see if breakfast was ready, I found Grandpa staring forlornly at the stove.

"Not the best day to replace a broken catch on the oven door," he was telling Bruno. "But never mind. Whole aircraft have flown tied together with chewing gum and string. I'm sure we'll be able to do something."

He strolled off toward his toolbox, singing "Having a Ball in Havana." As he went past the stove, its oven door crashed open.

"See?" Mum said. "That's what it's taken to doing every time I walk past it."

Grandpa slammed the oven door back up again and walked past a second time. It fell open again.

"We know the *problem,* Dad," Mum said. "What we're after here is the *solution.*"

If I took that tone with *my* dad, I'd be toast.

"I could strip it down and take a proper look at it," Grandpa offered.

Mum looked at him with suspicion. "Strip it down? And what does that mean?"

"It means completely taking it apart."

"You can't do that!" cried Mum. "It's Christmas morning! My turkey's supposed to be in there already. I can't have you and Bruno laying out bits of oven all over the floor! Think of something else! Quickly!"

"All right," said Grandpa. He tiptoed off toward his toolbox. The oven door stayed shut.

He turned to look at it.

"See that?" he asked me. "You try."

I tiptoed past the oven. It stayed shut.

"Now walk past perfectly naturally," he told me.

It's actually quite hard to walk past an oven perfectly naturally, when you've been told. (I expect Harry could have done it.) But anyhow, I did my best, and the door crashed down again.

"It's the catch," Grandpa told Mum.

"I know that," Mum said testily. "I would have known that anyway, given that the catch is broken in half, dead rusty, and hanging loose. Even if I had only a forkful of brain, those three giant clues would probably have been enough for me. But unless I was stone deaf as well, I would definitely have overheard you explaining to Bruno."

"Well," Grandpa said, "it's principally a matter of vibration. As long as the disturbance isn't too great, the catch can still cope. So until the hardware store opens after Christmas, that's your solution, I'm afraid."

"What is?" Mum asked him.

"Tiptoeing," Grandpa said. "Tiptoeing past it."

"Are you mad?" Mum asked. "Are you completely off your trolley, Dad? It's Christmas morning! I have sixteen people for lunch. How can I possibly tiptoe to and fro in front of my oven?"

Grandpa turned to Bruno. "Not very satisfactory, is it? But I rather think, Bruno, that it's the very best we can do for the moment."

Mum stared at Grandpa for a minute or two, then stalked off, humming. Grandpa watched her vanish into the larder, then turned and asked me anxiously, "What is that tune she's humming? I'm sure I recognize it, but I can't quite put a name to it."

"I'll go hum it to Dad," I said. "See if he remembers."

I went off and hummed at Dad, then asked him, "What's that I just hummed?"

"I do know it," said Dad. "Though I fear you're not giving it all the composer intended. It's called 'Careful with That Ax, Eugene!' and Tansy's mother always used to hum it when she was getting really, really, *really* mad at Grandpa."

I went back to the kitchen.

"Dad hasn't got a clue," I told Grandpa.

"Oh, well," said Grandpa. Then he turned to Bruno. "Want to come up to the bathroom and help me glue down that curling cork tile?"

Bruno wagged his tail and followed Grandpa out of the kitchen. I went to fetch Mum from the larder. "Sticky brown tape," I told her. "Shove in the turkey, then tape the oven closed. Each time you have to open the oven to baste the turkey, use fresh tape. After the lunch is over, you can make Grandpa wipe all the tape marks off with methylated spirit."

Mum stared at me. "Ralph!" she said. "You're a genius! An absolute genius! And, as a reward, I'm giving you a little present."

She reached in the kitchen drawer and took out the little joke wine-bottle stopper shaped like a man from the Australian outback with little corks on strings hanging from his hat. When you pull a tiny thread that hangs down between his shoulder blades, the corks start spinning round. I love it. I have loved it ever since Uncle Tristram brought it back from his year working in Melbourne. I've asked for it a million times, and she's always said she likes it too and I can't have it.

"There you are," she said. "All yours. Forever."

SNEAKWORM

Titania cheered up completely at breakfast, because there was lots of sneaking to be done.

"Mum-mee! Sylvester is eating with his mouth open."

"Mum-mee! Sylvia and Sylvester are sticking their tongues out at me."

"Mum-mee! Sylvia just called me a creepy little sneak-worm."

"Mum-mee! Ralph's just wiped his marmaladey fingers on the frill of his chair seat."

"I have not!" I countered. (Though I had.)

"Yes, you did. I *saw* you."

"You did *not.*"

"Quiet, Ralph," Mum warned. "Be polite to our visitors."

Great-granny crooked a thumb toward Titania and

said to my mother, "Left to myself, I'd take a rolled-up newspaper to that one."

"Are you speaking of my daughter?" Uncle Digby asked frostily.

"How should I know?" said Great-granny. "I can't be bothered to learn all their names. I'm talking about that great show-off down the end of the table who goes round dressed like a little cream puff with feet."

"That is a Fruzzy Anderson designer frock!" screeched Aunt Susan. "It cost nearly two hundred pounds!"

"I may not recognize a Fruzzy Anderson frock," said Great-granny. "But I recognize a giant waste of money when I see it."

"Yeah, Grandma!" muttered Uncle Tristram.

Mum heard, and gave Tristram one of those Don't-think-you're-too-big-to-be-sent-to-your-room looks. He shot Mum one of his So-what-are-you-going-to-do, sis? Throw-your-woolly-at-me? looks back.

"More toast, anyone?" asked my father. "We're having a spot of trouble with the oven door, but I'm reliably assured that the grill is still working."

"THIS LETTER IS FOR THE VERY PRETTY LITTLE GIRL"

When I came down from cleaning my teeth after breakfast, Mum was giving poor Grandpa a hard time in the hallway.

"What do you *mean*, 'just getting the picture rail back into true'? What did the doctor say only last week about you forever climbing up ladders and on chairs?"

"She said I wasn't to do it anymore," Grandpa admitted humbly. "She said my balance wasn't good enough, and I'd come over all dizzy."

"And what have I just caught you doing?"

"Climbing on a chair."

Mum hadn't finished shredding him. "That's *all* I want for Christmas, isn't it? A nice fresh corpse!"

I didn't mean to say it. It just slipped out. "*I* wouldn't mind a nice fre—"

Mum turned her steely look on me. I shut up straightaway, and she turned back to Grandpa. "You look flushed," she said. "Sit down on the chair for five minutes." She glanced at her watch. "I shall time you."

She went off to the kitchen. Grandpa sat on the chair, crooning a mournful song to Bruno.

"Your chee-eating hearrrrrrrrt
Will make you blooooooooooo—"

Instantly, Titania appeared in the doorway. "Are you having to sit down?"

Grandpa put up a fight. "Not for very long."

"Five minutes, I heard Aunty Tansy say."

"It's nearly over now," Grandpa said desperately.

Titania inspected her watch. "No, it isn't. There are at least four minutes left. I could sing you 'The Angel Who Flew to My Bedside.' It comes with its own little dance."

Uncle Tristram poked his head round the door. "She's like a vulture," he declared. "A puffy white designer-frocked vulture. She singles out the enfeebled and *swoops* on them unmercifully."

Titania ignored him. She was taking up her dance pose and opening her mouth.

An idea struck me. Digging in my pocket, I pulled out Uncle Tristram's "My dear, sweet child" letter.

Instantly, Uncle Tristram's head vanished.

I turned to Titania. "I have a letter for you."

She looked suspicious, but she shut her mouth.

"Early this morning," I told her, "I was down in the garden in that bit you call the magic dell. And I found this letter lying in a circle of red spotted mushrooms. And as I picked it up, I thought I heard a tiny voice, as if an elf were calling."

I did the tiny voice.

"This letter is for the very pretty little girl," it said.

It came out a bit Billy Goat Gruffish, so I tried the voice again, only tinier.

"This letter is for the very pretty little girl."

It still sounded a bit galumphing, for an elf. So I tried one last time.

"This letter is for the very pretty little girl."

Titania was still suspicious, you could tell, so I said, "Maybe he meant Sylvia."

That settled it. Glowering, Titania snatched the letter and stuffed it in her pocket. "No, it's for me. I'll read it after my song."

She took up her dance pose and opened her mouth again.

Grandpa said hastily, "Well, time's up! Come on, Bruno," and he rushed for the front door.

While Titania was wailing after him, I took the chance to rush off the other way, even though it was through the kitchen. And there I got caught, of course, and was made to sit down, and quietly do my fair share by peeling potatoes.

SORRY

Mum was still stuffing the turkey and working out timings for things in the oven when Dad came in, carrying the coal scuttle. He walked past the stove and the oven door crashed down.

"Sorry," he said, and slammed it up again.

"Jamie," Mum said to him, "could you just get those two big cartons of cream out of the fridge as you pass it, then rinse the Brussels sprouts under the tap for me and pull off any manky leaves."

"I'm a bit pushed, actually," said my father. "I still have to fill this coal bucket. Can't Ralph do it?"

"He's peeling spuds," said Mum. "You can actually see him sitting there doing it."

"One of the others?" Dad suggested. "I feel I'm already doing my full whack this morning."

Mum pulled her hand out of the turkey and straightened up. It seemed to me that there was a bit of a dangerous-looking Uncle Tristramy glint in her eyes.

"Would you like me to tell you about *my* full whack?" she asked him. "What I have done so far toward this Christmas?"

She leaned over the table. "So far this Christmas I have bought forty-seven presents for everyone from your grandmother to our cleaning lady's children. I have wrapped every single one of them in paper I myself went out to choose and purchase and carry home. And I have written a label for every single one of them and stuck it on."

"Sorry," said Dad.

"I have made two enormous Christmas puddings and two Christmas cakes, and also marzipan and icing. And I have gone out to find and buy tins large enough to keep them in."

"Sorry," Dad said again.

"I have driven across town to buy a seven-foot Christmas tree, lugged it across the car park and fought with that broken catch on the backseat I asked you to fix several weeks ago, finally managing to get everything down flat enough to shove the tree in. I have lugged the tree out of the back of the car onto the lawn at this end, and gone to the trouble of nagging you several times to set it up in the living room, and then even more times to set it up again each time it fell over because you'd made such a shoddy job of anchoring it in the bucket."

"Sorry," said Dad, blushing. "The problem was that—"

Mum just rode over him. "I also made an entire oyster costume for Ralph's part in the Christmas concert, a Star of Bethlehem out of tinfoil and tinsel for Albert's Nativity play after his mother came down with flu at a critical period in rehearsals, and a pretend postbox for Mrs. Henning's class's Christmas cards."

(That last one was my fault, but Dad said "Sorry" anyway.)

"I spent two entire days standing beside the boys while they teetered on ladders with holly and strings of cards and mistletoe and an assortment of weird decorations you claim to love to have around you at Christmas because they remind you of your happy childhood."

"Sorry," said Dad.

"Whereas I, who was raised in northern India, would just as soon have flown off to some beach in the Seychelles to relive some of *my* happy past Christmases," Mum reminded him.

"Sorry."

"I've written, addressed, stamped and posted seventy-three Christmas cards. I have attended two carol services, two school concerts and the pantomime you said you'd be coming to but had to miss because of a 'very important meeting' that later turned out to have been the office party."

"Oh, God! Sorry!" said Dad.

"I've washed all the best plates, since whoever washed them up after Christmas dinner last year—which I'll remind you was *you*—did a really rotten job and left streaks of dried cranberry sauce and gravy round the rims of more than half of them."

"Sorr-ee!" said Dad.

"I've staggered in from the supermarket with three heavy cartons of bottles because the person who said he would at least do that (which was *you*) left it so late it was getting to be a real worry."

"Sorry."

"I've made up seven extra beds, camp beds, futons and bedrolls, carefully thinking ahead so that our boys have ended up with all the torn, nasty, stained and faded sheets, and your elderly relations can swan about on our nice ones."

"Thank you," said Dad. "It's very thoughtful of—"

"Through all of this," Mum said, "I have carried on

with all the usual washing and ironing and cooking and cleaning and shopping and mending and chauffeuring people about."

"So you have," Dad said warmly.

"Not to mention my own job."

"Oh, dear."

"Now," Mum said, "I will ask you again, James. Would you please get out the Brussels sprouts and wash them in the colander under the tap, and pick off all the bad leaves for me?"

"Absolutely!" my dad said. And he put down the coal scuttle and rushed over to the vegetable rack.

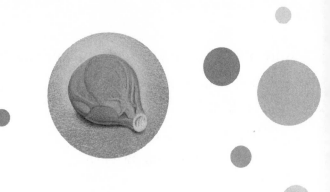

WALK

Halfway through the morning, Aunt Susan decided everyone had to go for a walk. Mum got out of it, claiming she had to keep an eye on the turkey. Dad got out of it claiming he had "things to do." Harry *nearly* got out of it by hiding behind the curtains in the living room.

And Sylvia and Sylvester and Titania were keen on the idea.

"Oh, goody!" said Titania. "As soon as we're safely away from the house, I can show everyone my lovely new Christmas Fairy dance."

She'd obviously read the letter. And believed it. But still I thought I'd take one last small risk, to save us from the Christmas Fairy dance.

I turned all cunning. "Did you know," I said, "that the

people who owned our house used to own all the land for miles around, so if, for example, someone ever cast a spell on us here at Green Gates House, whatever it said would count even if we went walking as far as Feltheringham."

(We never walk as far as Feltheringham, even when we're in the mood.)

Titania scowled and stamped her foot. That set off Sylvia, who stamped her foot as well, but in a puddle. Sylvester stamped in the next one, which was even deeper. And then, although Aunt Susan, me, Titania and Harry were already splattered, Sylvia and Sylvester stamped in the deepest yet.

"Children," Aunt Susan said (meaning Sylvia and Sylvester). "Please do try not to stamp in puddles."

Sylvia and Sylvester carried on stamping all along the walk. As we walked past the gates to the old park, Harry said,

"There used to be a zoo in there." (True.)

"It had a rhinoceros," I said. (True.)

"Very ugly," Harry added. (True.)

"Called Sylvester," I added. (Not true.)

Sylvester made a rhino charging noise. It was a noise to make a vampire fly back home, a noise to encourage a bogeyman to think twice, a noise to send a werewolf drooling in terror under the nearest bed.

"Good noise," said Sylvia, and she had a go at it too.

I could see startled faces appearing at windows as we walked by. Aunt Susan saw them as well.

"Please do try not to make that horrible noise, dears," she pleaded.

But they ignored her. The two of them kept at it, stamping through puddles and trumpeting horribly. Cunningly, Harry stayed ahead with Aunt Susan and talked up a storm each time we got to a corner, so that he managed to lead her round in a tight little circle and get back to our house quite soon.

"Oh, really!" said Aunt Susan when she realized. "How on earth did that happen?"

But Harry couldn't answer because he had already vanished, back into hiding.

I saw Mum's disappointed look as we went back inside. "That didn't take long."

"No," I said. "I think we'd all had enough of Sylvia and Sylvester splashing us with puddles and making their horrible noise."

"What horrible noise?" Dad asked me.

So I made it. (Since I was *asked*.)

Mum dropped the whisk she was holding, splattering droplets of double cream everywhere round her.

Dad grasped me firmly by the ears, stuck his face right

up to mine and told me firmly, "Listen, Buster. If you ever, *ever,* make that noise again within three miles of this house, I'll rip both of these ears of yours right off your head. Got it?"

"Got it," I assured him.

They made me clean up all the speckles of cream, too. I think Aunt Susan should maybe take parenting lessons from my father.

AHA!

U ncle Tristram stood in the doorway of the living room, admiring the huge pile of brightly wrapped presents heaped in the middle of the carpet.

"Is it the usual grabfest?" he asked cheerfully.

"No," Mum said firmly. "This year, we're doing it properly."

"What's 'properly'?"

Mum perched on the edge of the sofa. "Last year," she reminded him, "what with Sylvia and Sylvester being here, it just turned into a chaotic free-for-all."

"I rather liked that," I said wistfully.

Mum totally ignored me.

"It was awful." She shuddered. "Everyone just snatching up everything they could see with their name on the label, making huge loot piles and then ripping off the wrappings without even looking to see who the gift was from."

"Oh, come on," Uncle Tristram said. "It wasn't *that* bad."

"Yes, it was."

"Well, I think we should do it exactly that way again," Uncle Tristram said stubbornly.

"So do I," I said loudly, but once again Mum ignored me.

"I like that!" she was telling Uncle Tristram. "You were the one who complained most. You were the one who went round saying, 'Sylvia and Sylvester are not even reading the labels. I don't know why I bought both of them an expensive set of headphones. I might just as well have given each of them half a brick.' "

"Aha!" I said.

Uncle Tristram shot me a warning look and carried on arguing with his sister. "Nonetheless, I think we may as well just go ahead and do things the same way we did them last year."

Mum was mystified. "But *why*?"

Uncle Tristram spread his hands. "Tradition?"

"Tradition?" Mum laughed. "Well, so was bear-baiting. And going to laugh at lunatics. And men never pulling their weight in the kitchen."

Reminded, she dragged Uncle Tristram out to unpeel the tape on the oven door and check the turkey and potatoes to make sure they weren't burning.

CHRISTMAS
LUNCH

EVERYONE ROUNDED UP

Dad looked round the table. "I can't believe it! We finally have everyone rounded up and it's only two o'clock." Proudly, he counted. "Sixteen!" he said, and then looked baffled.

"It's Albert," I explained. "Albert's the extra one. He's been here all morning."

Dad turned to Mum. "Why?"

"I don't know," Mum said. "He just sort of dribbled over, and I didn't have the heart to send him home."

"I hope you warned him not to take any more unattended baths," Dad told her sternly. "Aren't his parents worried about him?"

"They know he's here," said Mum. "I made Ralph ring and tell them."

"What on earth are they doing," Dad asked the world in general, "that they don't want their only child around on Christmas Day?"

"When I rang, they were giggling," I told him. "And Teresa kept breaking off to say, 'Stop it, Lewis! You're spilling tea all down my nightie!' "

"Is Teresa that blond streak next door, with the legs?" asked Uncle Tristram.

"Shhh!" Mum said. "Not in front of Albert." She put on her bright voice. "I'm going to serve round the table starting at the far end," she said, "because that's much quicker and easier. Now, don't stand on ceremony. Once you've got your plate safely in front of you, tuck in before it gets cold."

She raised her voice for Great-aunt Ida. "Turkey, Aunt Ida?"

"Just a sliver, dear," whimpered Aunt Ida. "You know that, when it comes to poultry, I might as well book into the little girls' room from now until New Year."

Dad passed her the baby Brussels sprouts. "Now, do take these one at a time," he warned. "What with your weak wrist, and all that."

Mum was too far away to kick him so she gave him a look. Then she moved on to Uncle Tristram. "Dark meat or white?"

"Whichever comes in bigger lumps," he said. "Just shovel it onto the plate, sis. I'm starving."

Great-aunt Ida shuddered gently beside him.

Mum gave Uncle Tristram a perfectly normal-sized helping and moved on to Great-granny.

"Did you know the bird?" Great-granny asked.

"What, personally?" asked Mum.

"Yes."

"As it happens, no."

"Unless choosing it from ten thousand others in Tesco can be considered an introduction," my dad said.

"Then I won't, dear. I'll just stick with sausages, thank you."

"We haven't met the pig socially, either," my dad said. "Does that not put you off?"

Titania stared. "Is sausage made from pig, then?"

"Yes."

"From dead pig's bottom?"

"Put like that," Dad said, "it does sound a shade unappetizing. But, yes, that's more or less what it is."

"If you're *lucky*," I added, because I'd watched a program on telly about the bits they *really* use to make pork sausage, and they weren't even as nice as pig's bottom.

"I think we've had enough of this conversation," Mum said in her bright voice. "Digby?"

"Can't," Uncle Digby said. "I'm on a special diet. Vegetables only for me."

Aunt Miriam was avoiding fats, so she stuck to a slice of turkey without skin and a few Brussels sprouts. Sylvia had only stuffing. Sylvester had only turkey and sausage. Then the two of them spent the next ten minutes noisily trading foodstuffs until both had some turkey, some stuffing, and a sausage.

Mum did Grandpa next. Grandpa confided to me once that he no longer really cares for eating anything that has a face and feet. But he still took some turkey because he knows Bruno likes it, and he could pass the time feeding him under the table.

Mum got to Harry and me.

"Just burnt spuds, please," said Harry when she offered him potatoes.

Mum laid her serving spoon very deliberately down on the best cloth. "None of the potatoes are *burnt,* Harry," she said. "It's just that some of them are nicely browned."

"Just nicely browned ones, then, please," said Harry. (He knows the warning signs.) Mum picked up her serving spoon and, when she'd sorted out Harry's plate, she turned to me.

I wondered how best to put it.

"Just nicely *not* browned ones, please," I ended up saying.

"Mum-mee!" sneaked Titania. "Ralph's being cheeky to his mother."

"No, I am not!"

"You *are*."

"I'm *not*!"

"Mum-mee! Ralph's shouting at me down the table."

"No, I am *not*!"

"Yes, you are!"

"No, I'm *not*!"

"Mum-*mee*!"

Uncle Tristram kindly rescued me. "Funny," he said to Titania. "I once heard about a really weird fairy spell that was cast on anyone who kept arguing in this house through Christmas lunch."

Titania shut up at once.

Mum got round to Uncle Geoffrey. "Any preferences?"

"No, no," he said. "Shovel it on. Whatever."

"Sausages?"

"The more the merrier."

"Stuffing?"

"Ooh, lovely. I'm happy to eat as much as you can give me."

Mum didn't even ask Albert. She just passed him a plate of cut-up sausages and potatoes and one small Brussels sprout. The minute the plate was put down in front of him, Albert picked up the Brussels sprout as if it were something really unpleasant and dropped it on Uncle Geoffrey's plate.

"I'll take some of your bits of sausage as well, if they're too much for you," Geoffrey said hopefully.

I heard Dad muttering, "I'm sure nobody doubts it," but I don't think Mum can have caught it because she went on to Aunt Susan without giving him one of her looks.

"Is the turkey organic?" asked Aunt Susan.

"It was supposed to be," said Mum. "But then the farmer let us down. So it's not."

"I won't, then, if you don't mind."

"Stuffing?"

Aunt Susan put on a pained face. "Oh, I don't think so, Tansy."

Mum didn't even bother offering sausages.

"Roast potatoes?"

"Were they basted with turkey fat? I expect they were. I think I'll pass on those."

"You'll have the Brussels sprouts, perhaps?"

"Are *they* organic?"

"Yes," Mum lied. (She told Dad afterward that it was either lying or throwing the turkey carcass at Aunt Susan, and Dad agreed she had chosen The Better Path.)

"That's everyone served at last, then," Mum said. "Phew!"

She was about to serve herself when Uncle Tristram's empty plate arrived in front of her, passed up from the end of the table.

"Are there seconds?" he was asking hopefully.

Mum went red in the face. She turned to Dad. "Well, I admit it. You were right," she said.

"What about?" Dad said, mystified.

"When I was worrying about the food. You came up behind me and put your arms around me and said, 'Don't give it a moment's thought, Tansy. You can drive yourself into the ground cooking for that lot, and at the end you'll realize you might as well have been feeding them *hay*.' "

"Ha, ha!" Dad said. "Very amusing!" He turned to everyone staring around the table. "I never said that, of course. Tansy's making it up. Very funny, Tansy. Very funny."

I don't think for a moment that anyone believed him.

THE SOUND OF SOBBING

I heard the sound of sobbing through their bed-room door. "Buck up, Tans!" Dad kept saying. "Stiffen the mush! At least it only happens once a year."

Mum said through sniffles, "I'm not doing it next year. I want that thoroughly understood. Next year, we go abroad. Promise?"

"We'll talk about it after they've all gone," Dad tried to soothe her.

"No," she said. "I'm not coming down till you've promised."

"I promise," said Dad, a shade too easily.

I heard a drawer opening, then a sort of scrabbling.

"Go on," she ordered him. "Write it down."

"What?"

"I, James Henry Mountfield, promise that I will take my wife and children, and no one else, abroad for a holiday all through next Christmas and New Year."

I held my breath. There was a bit of a silence, then a sigh, and then a scratching noise, and then:

"Will that do?"

More silence while Mum checked. Then:

"Date it, please."

He obviously dated it.

"Right. Now sign it. In blood."

"In *blood*?"

"Yes. In blood. Or I'm not coming down."

"But it's the opening of the presents next. You can't miss the opening of the presents."

"I can miss anything I want," she warned him. "I can have a three-day migraine and miss the whole damn lot. I could suddenly find I have a headache that only begins to clear up the moment I hear the last of their cars pulling away."

She meant it, you could tell. Dad knew it too.

"All right," he said. There was a longer silence, then a

yelp, and then more silence. Later came the sound of them kissing.

I slid away. Not too long after, they came down again. Mum had a much more cheerful look on her face, and Dad had a brand-new plaster on his finger.

A SHORT APPEAL

I followed Dad into the living room to find Great-granny jabbing the wrong end of the remote control over and over again at the telly.

"Your set is broken."

"No, it's not," said Dad, and reached down to switch it on. The Queen was sitting in a large embroidered armchair, chatting about her journeys round the Commonwealth.

Great-granny snorted. "Luxury travel! And all at Joe Taxpayer's expense!"

"Do you not want it, then?" Dad asked pleasantly. "Shall I switch it off?"

"Yes!" said Titania, forgetting the spell for a moment. "Switch it off and I'll sing a little song for everyone instead."

What with Dad being there (and not stupid), I didn't dare remind Titania about her letter from Santa. But Great-granny came to the rescue.

"You can stand there till you rot," she said, "but no one's going to ask *you* to sing."

"*I'll* sing, then," Albert offered. "Except I'm not going to sing 'Away in a Manger' because I *don't* love the Little Lord Jesus, and I *don't* think he has a sweet head."

"We'll hear the Queen out first, shall we?" Dad said, to settle the argument. "Then we can hear both of you singing."

"I see you've turned mollycoddling spoiled brats into an art form," said Great-granny.

Uncle Digby spoke up from the chair in which we all thought he was fast asleep. "Please don't be unpleasant about my precious daughter."

"She may be your precious daughter," said Great-granny, "but the general opinion is that she's bossy and charmless."

Uncle Digby prized himself out of his armchair and stormed out.

"Now look what you've done, Natasha," scolded my father.

Great-granny sniffed. "If the man can't accept good child-rearing advice, honestly given, then I'm afraid he must fend for himself." She pulled her horses' heads scarf more tightly round her shoulders. "In any event," she confided, "I shall be crossing his entire family off my Christmas card list."

After the Queen finished, there was a short appeal on behalf of battered children. We heard a scrabbling, and all turned round to see Great-granny digging in her bag for a pen and her checkbook.

"A very worthwhile cause," she kept on saying. "And, after all, it is Christmas."

I thought it was a bit unlike her. But only Dad had the brains to suss it out.

"No, no, Natasha," he warned. "It isn't a help line to advise people how to do it. It's a help line to try and prevent them."

Great-granny looked up. "Really?" You could tell she was astonished. She stuffed her checkbook back in her bag. "I can't for the life of me imagine who might want to support that."

CHRISTMAS AFTERNOON

OPENING THE PRESENTS

So finally, *finally,* it was time for the opening of the presents. The people who had lost the toss at lunch trooped back after all the clearing and washing up and drying and putting things away in cupboards. Albert followed everyone into the living room and settled on a cushion on the floor next to Uncle Tristram.

"That child would give you the eyes out of his head to play marbles with," Great-granny said to Uncle Tristram.

"He has taken a bit of a shine to me, hasn't he?" Uncle Tristram said proudly. "I think I probably have a way with children."

"You don't have a way with children," Mum said. "It's just that they know that, if they sit by you, sooner or later they'll hear something they shouldn't."

She settled Great-granny and Great-aunt Ida down in the only comfy chairs. She made Harry give Grandpa the bit of the sofa he'd bagged, because Grandpa had "old bones." She separated Sylvia and Sylvester and put them where they couldn't easily make any more faces at each other. She pretended not to notice that Titania was shifting her stool along in front of the mirror so that every time she rearranged her frock or patted her hair she could admire her own reflection. She stopped Uncle Tristram from taking his shirt off to show me the scar on his shoulder from when he fell down a cliff path on the Isle of Wight.

And then, finally, *finally,* she said we were ready.

The great pile of shiny wrapped presents sat in the middle of the floor, glistening and winking. I could hardly *wait.* I was *bursting* with anticipation.

"Look at it!" said Aunt Susan. "It's disgusting, isn't it? A monument to greed and empty Western values. It makes me quite ill to look at it!"

"Would you like to go home now, then?" Dad offered hopefully.

"James!" Mum said sharply. She smiled her "bright" smile. "Right, then," she carried on. "These are the new rules." And she started to explain.

It all sounded a bit complicated.

"Do you suppose this is how they do it in Wormwood Scrubs?" said Uncle Tristram.

"What's Wormwood Scrubs?" asked Albert.

"It's a big prison," said Uncle Tristram. "Dead strict." He looked at Mum and added defensively, "See? That was just educational. No reason on earth why Albert shouldn't know that."

Mum finished up the rules. "And so, to recap, no *grabbing*. Understood?"

Everyone nodded glumly. So then we started. Titania won the toss, and, jumping daintily over Sylvester's deliberately stuck-out foot, smirked at herself in the mirror as she picked out a present.

She studied the label prettily with her head on one side and then handed the present to Uncle Tristram with a little bob—not quite a curtsy.

"It's for you."

Uncle Tristram read the label. "It's from Great-aunt Ida," he told everybody.

"This is going to take *ages*," grumbled Harry.

Uncle Tristram looked across to Great-aunt Ida. "Thank you," he said to her. "Thank you very much."

"You're most welcome," said Great-aunt Ida.

"Doing it this way is going to take for*ever*," moaned Harry.

"Thank you again, Aunt Ida," said Uncle Tristram. "I'm going to unwrap your gift now."

Mum gave him a Don't-push-your-luck-any-further look.

Uncle Tristram tore off the wrappings. Inside was a box of hankies with embroidered parrots in the corners.

"I gave Great-aunt Ida those last year," I told him.

I thought I said it quietly enough, but Dad still aimed a slap at my head. Grandpa put on his glasses. "I remember those. I bought those in Patagonia. I thought I gave them to you as a birthday present, Tristram."

"You did," Tristram told him. "Ages ago. Then I gave them to James and Tansy as a thank-you-for-having-me gift."

"They were in the cupboard for ages," said Harry.

"Is that why you told me I could have them," I asked Mum, "to give to Great-aunt Ida last year?"

"The old way of doing things did have at least one advantage," Dad pointed out. "In all that ugly free-for-all grabbing, there was at least no chance to discuss the provenance of each and every gift."

"What's provenance?" asked Albert.

"Where it came from," said Uncle Tristram. "In this case, who's given it to whom before."

"Does that child *never* stop asking questions?" asked Great-granny.

"At least he remembers the answers," I told her. "Along with everything else he hears. He practically knows the whole poem 'The Walrus and the Carpenter,' just from hearing Mum test me on my cues for being eaten." I thought, since whatever present she'd given me must be already in the pile, I might as well push my luck a bit. "*And* he gets all our names right."

"Tristram," Mum said hastily. "Since you got the last gift, you get to choose the next present from the pile."

"Is that quite fair?" asked Grandpa. "After all, Tristram already has one."

"He's not *having* the next one," Mum explained to Grandpa. "He simply gets to choose it from the pile."

"I might be lucky," Uncle Tristram argued. "I might just happen to pick out one that's for myself."

"Then I hope you'll have the grace and sensitivity to put it back on the pile straightaway," said my mother.

"Oh, no! It'll be Boxing Day before we get finished at this rate!" wailed Harry.

Dad aimed a slap at Harry's head as well. To cheer him up, Uncle Tristram rooted through the pile until he found a present labeled "Harry" and handed it over. "Here you are."

Harry started to rip off the paper.

94

"Who's it from?" Mum prompted in her warning voice.

Harry stopped ripping and inspected the label. "I can't read this writing. I'm not even sure it says Harry."

Uncle Tristram leaned over him to look at it as well. "That is definitely a 'Harry,'" he declared after a moment.

"How do you make that out?"

"Well, that's a capital *H*."

"No, it isn't."

"I think you'll find it is."

"Suppose you're wrong. I will have opened someone else's present."

"No, you won't," said Uncle Tristram. "I know for a fact this present is for you."

"How?"

"Because I bought it."

"Oh, ta!" said Harry, and went back to ripping. Inside was a plastic pouch that said THEATRE WORLD in huge letters. And out of that Harry slid an enormous false black beard.

"That's brilliant!" I said, deadly envious.

"Don't worry," Uncle Tristram told me. "I got you one too."

"Mum-mee!" sneaked Titania. "Uncle Tristram's spoiling all the surprises."

"Not all of them," said Uncle Tristram, and he winked at me because we knew about the wrapped-up halves of brick and nobody else did.

Harry put on his beard at once. It hooked over his ears and went down to his feet.

"Very stylish," said Great-granny.

"Recently, somebody looking very much like that floated right past my window," Great-aunt Ida confided.

"I should make sure to keep your window very tightly closed in future," Dad advised her.

"Brilliant!" said Harry, through a mouthful of beard, though it came out so muffled that you could barely hear it.

"You're going to look very fetching in the Christmas photos," Mum said.

"Rasputin's turn to pick a present," Dad said.

Albert looked up at Uncle Tristram. "Who's Rasputin?"

"He was a Russian with a beard like that," said Uncle Tristram. "He was cruel, cunning and evil. To kill him, his enemies at court put enough poison to kill a horse into his grub at dinner, but he was so tough that they still had to shoot him about seventeen times and then kick his twitching body into the canal."

"See?" Mum said. "What did I tell you? That's why he likes sitting next to you."

"It's all educational," argued Uncle Tristram.

Harry tried picking the next present through his waterfall of beard. It took a bit of time, but finally he managed to grasp one. I recognized the shape of it. It was half-a-brick shaped.

"It's very heavy," he said. "It's for Sylvia. And there's nothing on the label to say who it's from."

I really like Uncle Tristram, so I kept quiet. But he had obviously decided that the best thing was to defend himself in advance.

"Nobody bothered to read the labels last year," he reminded everyone. "Everyone just pitched in and grabbed."

"I didn't," said Aunt Susan.

"Neither did I," said Titania. "I thanked everyone, and gave them a pretty curtsy and danced them a little dance."

"So you did," said my dad, remembering.

"Well, *some* people just grabbed," said Uncle Tristram. "And never even bothered to look to see who'd given them their headph—" He knew he'd blown his cover then, but he pressed on regardless. "Whatever. They certainly never went to the trouble to try to find out who had been so very generous, or write a letter to thank him. So that person who bought them both a nice gift last year could hardly be blamed, could he, if this year he doesn't get the world's best present for the two who didn't even thank him."

Everyone stared at him, trying to decipher this.

"Everyone else gets a beard," Uncle Tristram added.

"I thanked you," said Titania. "Have you given me a beard?"

"Rest assured," said Uncle Tristram. "In that pile somewhere is a beard for you."

Titania burst into tears.

"Mum-meee!" she sobbed. "Uncle Tristram has bought me a horrible, horrible, horrible present!"

Harry was quicker off the mark than I was. "I'll have your beard if you don't want it. I don't mind having a spare. I'll swap you something for it."

Titania switched off her crying like a tap. "What else have you got?" she demanded.

"I don't know yet, do I?" Harry said. "This is all taking so *long.*"

"Unwrap your present, dear," Mum told Sylvia.

Sylvia unwrapped it. It was half a brick.

"Who is it from?" she asked.

Nobody owned up.

He'd rescued me at lunchtime. So I decided to rescue him back.

"It's art," I announced. "It was very, very expensive. I was with Uncle Tristram when he bought it. The man in the art gallery shop said that it was created by the brother of the famous dress designer, Fruzzy Anderson."

"Well, there you are!" said Great-granny. "Daylight robbery obviously runs in the family. Look no further than Little Miss Cream Puff's frocks."

"Please don't call my daughter that," Digby reproved her.

"What?"

"Little Miss Cream Puff."

"I'll call your daughter what I choose," said Great-granny. "After hearing what you called me the moment you left the breakfast table."

"What was that?" I asked.

"No!" Mum said sharply. But it was too late. Sylvester had already repeated it.

"Uncle Digby called her 'a malevolent old trout.' "

"What's malevolent?" asked Albert.

"Evil," explained Uncle Tristram.

"Like Rasputin!" said Albert.

"See?" Uncle Tristram crowed at Mum. "I told you it was educational."

Mum stood up. "Who wants a cup of tea?"

Some did. Some didn't. Some thought it was too early. Some said they'd been fearing that she'd never ask.

"While I'm out of the room," Mum said, "do feel free to carry on opening the presents any way you choose. I'll leave you to it and be back in a few minutes."

She was gone half an hour. By the time she came back with the tea tray, the worst was over. We were just mopping up the little presents round the edges, and most of the swapping was over. Titania had forgiven Uncle Tristram and given him her beard in return for some castanets someone had given Great-aunt Ida years ago and she'd only just passed on. But Sylvia wouldn't swap her half brick for anything, not for *anything*, even though, out of guilt (and fear of Mum), Uncle Tristram had offered her a whole heap of scented bath seeds, some socks and a diabolo, and Sylvester offered everything he had, except his own half brick. (I think he was ready to have a go at our new shed, and though adults can say to you, "Please put down those bits of brick at once," you can't really be told off for carrying two presents.)

The person who'd done best was Albert. He hadn't even been invited, and still he had a whole heap of things that no one wanted and they couldn't swap.

"That's the spirit of Christmas for you," my father

said expansively. "Opening one's home and hearth to a stranger."

"That's the spirit of sherry talking," Great-granny said tartly. "That child is scarcely a stranger. Why, only this morning I came across him lolling in my bath."

"Albert, what did I tell you about that?" Mum scolded.

THE CHRISTMAS QUIZ

S o that's how everything was before we started the Christmas Quiz. (This was what got me sent up here. On my own. Alone. On Christmas Day. Even though none of it was my fault.)

I blame Aunt Susan. It was her idea. "While we're all sitting here after that lovely cake and all that excitement, why don't we exercise our minds?"

It sounded ghastly. Everyone ignored her.

"Have a little quiz."

That sounded better. One or two of them looked up.

"What sort of quiz?"

"Will there be prizes?"

"General knowledge," said Aunt Susan.

"That won't be fair," whined Titania. "If the quiz is on

general knowledge, then it's bound to be won by one of the grown-ups."

"Or Albert," Uncle Tristram said smugly.

"Fantabbydozy!" said Albert. (He heard that from me.)

"We could have it on something the children know as much about as the adults," my father suggested.

"Like what?" said Harry.

We all had a ponder. I know a lot more than any adult about the garden. And the cupboard under the stairs. And what's in the attic. And which of next door's apple trees is the best. And my school. And what's sold in the chocolate machine on the corner.

And that's about it.

"I know!" said Aunt Susan. "Let's have a quiz on the family."

Titania started whining. "But all the grown-ups have been in the family for soooo much longer. One of them is bound to win."

"I know," I said. "Let's make it just on the bits that everyone has been here for. Let's make it a Christmas Visit Quiz."

That is ALL I SAID.

Dad looked at Titania. "Would you consider that fair? All questions to be about our Christmas Eve and Christmas Day?"

"Have you had to whine much for *everything* you've wanted?" Great-granny asked Titania.

Titania ignored her. She told my father, "We can only have questions on what happened yesterday, Christmas Eve, and today, Christmas Day, until now." She looked at her watch. "Up till six-fifteen exactly."

"Obviously," my father said patiently. "Or it wouldn't be a quiz but a test of soothsaying." He turned to Albert. "That means telling the future," he explained, and Uncle Tristram looked hurt, as if his job had been stolen from him.

"I'll start," said Great-granny. "Who has taken my horses' heads scarf from the top of my dresser?"

She stared at Titania, who turned red and said, "I only borrowed it."

"Well, fetch it *back*."

Titania scuttled off.

"While she is doing that," Great-granny said, "I'm going to ask another. Who was it left my soap in the bath till it went so soggy that it was useless?"

This time, she stared at Albert.

"Natasha," my mother said gently, "I'm not sure this is quite in the spirit of a friendly family quiz."

"I have more questions," said Great-granny. "But since they appear to be unwelcome, I will save them till later."

Dad covered the uneasy silence by going to the corner cupboard and taking out a pad of paper and pencils and colored pens. "Here you are," he said, handing them round. "We'll make it sixteen questions, so everyone gets to ask one. We won't count Great-granny's first two, since they were just a practice run. We'll start off now. The first person to answer the question correctly gets to put a tick on their sheet of paper."

Titania flounced back through the door, watching herself in the mirror as she waved the horses' heads scarf around her head as though she were a Gypsy dancer.

"How strange," Uncle Tristram warned her. "Suddenly I feel a sort of magic in the air, as if some old spell were stirring."

Titania sat down, fast.

"Bags be first," I said. "Who told the best joke ever?"

(I was thinking of Brown Paper Pete.)

"Youngest first," said my father. He waited till Titania had put on her What—*me*? astonished look and taken a breath, and then said: "Albert!"

Albert looked happily round the room. "Who fed Bruno lots and lots and lots of turkey under the table?"

Mum said, "Oh, really! How infuriating!" Then she said, "I'm not even going to *ask*." Then she said, "I honestly don't want to know who could be so inconsiderate and maddening." Then she said, "All right! Own up. Who was it?"

"*You* can't ask," Albert reproved her. "It's *my* question."

"Ask it again," Mum said grimly.

Albert asked it again, but nobody came up with an answer.

"Go on, then," Mum said to Albert. "Tell us."

"No, don't!" said Grandpa.

"You!" said Mum. "I can't believe it, Dad! After the fuss you always used to make if Susan or I ever did it! And what a bad example! Honestly! Not to mention the waste of good food that could have gone into tomorrow's risotto."

"Oh, not risotto!" Uncle Geoffrey said. "I can't abide risotto."

"Do feel free to leave *before* lunch," my father said kindly.

"Next question!" Mum said hastily.

"Is it me now?" I asked. "Who told the greatest joke *ever* over the whole two days?"

"Uncle Geoffrey," my father said softly, so only Uncle Geoffrey and the people between them heard. Uncle Geoffrey went scarlet and scowled at him furiously. Dad looked dead smug, as if he'd paid him out royally for not liking risotto.

"*Did* you have a good one?" I asked him, thinking we could hear them both and then everyone could vote for mine.

"No," he said firmly.

Dad and Uncle Tristram sniggered.

Aunt Susan called over from the sofa, "What's all this about? Has Geoffrey got some really good joke he hasn't told me?"

"You couldn't call it 'good,' " giggled Tristram. "Though it is *funny.*"

Uncle Geoffrey was panicking. "Shut up!" he hissed at Uncle Tristram. Then, turning to Aunt Susan, he said as lightly as he could, "Well, even if I had, dear, it's no use asking because I'm afraid I've completely forgotten it."

"*We* haven't," warned my father.

"I could tell mine anyway," I offered hopefully. "This man goes into a bar in the Wild West—"

"For heaven's sake, give the boy his point," said Great-granny. "I really can't face hearing his damn-awful joke twice."

"Please don't swear in front of Albert," said Uncle Tristram.

Great-granny gave him the sort of look Rasputin

probably turned on the people trying to poison and shoot and drown him.

"I'm going to slide in one more teensy question of my own," she said. "Who was it throwing potatoes at Tansy's cat?"

Mum looked reproachfully at Uncle Tristram.

"Sorry," he muttered. "Couldn't help it. Suddenly got the urge."

Mum smiled. "I understand. And was that before, or after, you got the urge to make the list entitled 'Ten Things I Hate Most About Great-granny'?"

Uncle Tristram put his head in his hands. Mum turned to Great-aunt Ida.

"Aunt Ida, it's your turn. Ask everyone a question. Any question, so long as it's about today or yesterday."

Great-aunt Ida cocked her head to one side and asked us all, "Who was it who just floated past the window?"

Dad sighed. I heard him muttering to Mum, "I shall be very relieved indeed, you know, to get her safely back in the Home."

"I know!" said Titania, out to grub for points. "It was the vicar!"

She sat there. "Prove me wrong," her face said.

Great-aunt Ida was delighted. "That's right, dear! It was the vicar."

There was silence. No one was sure quite how to call Titania a liar and a cheat without calling Great-aunt Ida a loony. So no one said anything at all till Mum said to Titania, "Are you quite sure, dear?"

"Yes, I am," said Titania, and put her first tick on her paper.

"I saw him too," said Albert. "He was huge and lumpy-looking, with funny eyes, and hair that stuck out all over, and he looked as if he'd been drinking blood and severing people's arms off in Snowville."

The vicar looks a bit like that as well. So, once again, no one felt confident about arguing.

"Let's go on to the next question," Dad said. "Sylvester?"

"Why was Aunt Tansy crying in the bedroom this afternoon?" Sylvester asked.

"This quiz isn't working out at all right," my dad said.

"I was just tired," Mum told Sylvester. "Just for a moment. And I had a little headache." She gazed round cheerfully. "My point, I think?"

"No," said Sylvester. "You can't have a point."

"Why not?"

"Because that's not the answer."

"How do *you* know?"

"Because I heard Ralph telling Harry that Uncle

James had to sign in blood that you're going on holiday next year instead of having Christmas."

Mum looked at me as if I had betrayed her utterly.

"I only told *Harry*," I defended myself. "He is my *brother*. And even then, I only *whispered*." I turned on Sylvester. "You must have been sneaking about, eavesdropping."

"Let's all play Monopoly instead," said my father.

"No," Uncle Tristram said. "Let's not stop now. I'm beginning to enjoy this. I'll ask the next question. Geoffrey, why do you never bring a bottle when you come to stay with people?"

Uncle Geoffrey was outraged. "What do you mean? Miriam and I bought everyone a present."

"And everyone gave you one back. But, meantime, there are four of you stuffing your faces at every meal, and whole swaths of repairs to be paid for as soon as Sylvia and Sylvester have finally finished chipping the furniture and treading food into rugs and spilling coffee down sofas and leaving drink-can rings on polished furniture."

I would have mentioned my owl, but my dad got his gripe in first. "Not to mention the upcoming vet bills."

Uncle Tristram spread his hands. And fixing damage to the shed and the greenhouse. And yet you never bring so much as a bottle of sherry."

110

I took revenge on Sylvester. "Or your own bread rolls to hurl around in the garden."

"I know the answer to the question!" shouted Sylvia. "Daddy's saving money to buy an investment property in London."

"What's an investment property?" asked Albert.

"It's a house you don't need," said Uncle Tristram, "in which you keep someone who pays you huge amounts of money."

"Which you then keep entirely to yourself," muttered my father.

Uncle Geoffrey overheard. "All right," he said rattily. "I'm going to ask a question back now. If I have such a reputation for not flinging my money around, when can I expect to be paid back the thousand pounds that I so generously lent you two years ago?"

"I definitely think we should be playing some other game," said my father.

But Aunt Miriam has a temper when she's riled as well.

"*And* my pearl earrings," she added.

"Sorry?" said Mum.

"My pearl earrings," insisted Aunt Miriam. "The ones I lent you back in October, for that dance, and haven't seen back yet."

Mum shrugged. "Oh, did you want them back, particularly?"

"I should think so," said Aunt Miriam. "Since they were a very special anniversary present from Geoffrey."

Mum looked at Geoffrey. Then she looked at Aunt Miriam. I watched the color draining out of her face.

"They weren't *real* pearls, were they?"

"Of *course* they were real pearls. What did you *think* they were?"

Mum looked quite white. "Well, pretend ones, of course, just like everyone else wears."

Aunt Miriam put on a look that as good as said, "So you *say* . . ."

Mum saw it. "Miriam," she said coldly, "are you suggesting that I realized those were real pearls, and was secretly hoping I could keep them?"

"No," said Aunt Miriam. "I'm simply suggesting that you've been forgetting to give them back to me for quite a long time."

Mum sprang to her feet. "I'll fetch them now," she said, and spun on her heel so hard, she practically left sparks on the carpet.

We all sat in silence, waiting. I would have done my bit to try to start up a conversation, but I suddenly felt uneasy.

Pearls . . .

It was ringing a bit of a bell, but I couldn't quite remember.

Mum was away a long time. Long enough for Dad to crack from the strain of the waiting and offer Uncle Geoffrey a drink.

Uncle Geoffrey put his hand over the top of his glass. "No, thank you. I rather think I may be driving shortly."

That's when I realized it was getting serious. For some mysterious reason I couldn't understand, the vague, uneasy feeling I'd had at the thought of pearls turned into a terrible grip in my stomach.

Mum came back with a slight flush on her face, holding her jewelry box. "Just carry on," she said, "while I sort through this lot again. They have to be in here somewhere."

We carried on being quite silent while she searched.

In the end, she admitted it. "They're not here."

Aunt Miriam's silence got louder.

"I can't think where they are!" wailed Mum. "It's not as if James or the boys would have borrowed them!" She looked round, mystified. "Who else would want to wear pearls?"

"An oyster?" said Albert, beside me.

And that's when it all came flooding back.

Nobody heard him except me. They were all busy answering Mum's question by staring at Titania. I suppose they were remembering the head scarf. I expect they were thinking that anyone brave enough to creep into Great-granny's bedroom and borrow her horses' heads scarf without permission was probably foolhardy enough to organize a bank raid, let alone take a pearl or two out of an aunt's jewelry box.

But I was remembering something different. I was remembering putting on my oyster costume for the Christmas concert and thinking it was rather drab. Don't get me wrong now. Mum had done her best. But it was just two giant circles of gray cardboard, taped together. Sort of round. Sort of gray.

And sort of boring.

I suppose I was jealous. You see, the Walrus had his brilliant droopy mustache and his long flippery tail. The Carpenter had a squat black crumpled hat and an old-fashioned fob watch on a chain and his brightly patterned waistcoat. And the only thing I could imagine an oyster might ever have in the way of frivolity was—

A pearl.

So I'd borrowed the earrings. Just for the one performance. I hadn't asked Mum before taking them because she was rushing round the house looking for car keys while she phoned Teresa to tell her she was sending Albert home at once and shrieking at me to hurry because we were going to be late and Mrs. Hathaway would kill us.

I meant to tell her as soon as we were in the car, but she started on one of her inquisitions.

"Have you got the right shoes?"

"On my feet."

"And your oyster shells? Both of them?"

"Yes, Mum. Albert counted to two for me."

"Don't you be fresh with me. Have you got your woolly tights on?"

I have my pride. "*Your* woolly tights."

"And that disgusting smelly stuff Mrs. Hathaway gave you to slick back your hair?"

"Hair gel. Yes, Mum. In my pocket."

And by then we were in the car park. Mum had a ticket so she was swept off by the third-year ushers through the front doors, and I was ordered round the back by Mr. Harris. In the changing rooms I fastened the earrings onto my circles of shell, one on the front and one on the back, so that whichever way I was facing, anyone would know I was an oyster with a pearl.

Then Mrs. Hathaway came along. "What are these earrings on your oyster shell?"

"They're my pearls," I said proudly.

"Take them off," she said. "Oysters' pearls grow on the inside."

You don't mess with Mrs. Hathaway. So I took off the pearl earrings and stuffed them down the front of Mum's woolly tights, where no one would see them but I would know they were there. Mrs. Hathaway is always exhorting us to "give that little ten percent extra in performance, as if you know a whole lot more about the character you're playing than you are letting on."

So I tried to act like an oyster who knows that, deep inside, he has two precious pearls. I put on a rather dreamy look, a bit like Titania going into her "Princess Waking Up from a Lovely Dream" dance. I hoped it told the audience I was the only person in the world who knew my wonderful secret. Teresa next door went round acting daft and smiley in the same way as well, before admitting to Mum last week she was pregnant again.

I modeled my performance on theirs.

And got in big trouble for it, since afterward, as I told you at the start, everyone complained I looked much, much too happy while I was being eaten.

But now it was obviously time to have a go at acting again. Mum was still rooting through the jewelry box, getting more and more frantic, and everyone else was now trying *not* to look at Titania.

I spread my hands, and let my mouth fall open, and tried to look as if I'd only just tuned in.

"Oh, *those* earrings!" I said. "Are we talking about *those* earrings?"

They all stopped not looking at Titania and started definitely looking at me.

"Do you know where they are?" said Mum.

"Upstairs," I said. (Safe guess. I'm not allowed to leave my clobber from school lying around downstairs.) "I'll go and fetch them."

At the door, I made a little plea.

"Don't just sit waiting. This might take a bit of time. Just carry on enjoying the quiz while I'm up there."

My dad's hand would have reached me that time, but I moved too fast.

UPSTAIRS - AND DOWN AGAIN

I knew I hadn't remembered to take the earrings out of the tights. I'd just come home in a sulk from all the complaints about my performance. ("Ten percent extra!" said Mrs. Hathaway. "Not ninety percent grinning halfwit!")

I'd shoved the oyster shells out of sight in my closet, then rolled the woolly tights in a ball and tossed them in my laundry pile.

Where they weren't to be found any longer.

I crept downstairs again and lurked behind the doorway to the sitting room, hoping to catch Mum's eye. I was not *eavesdropping*. I just couldn't help *overhearing*.

"That boy's been nothing but trouble since Christmas

began," Aunt Miriam was complaining. "*And* it was his idea to have the quiz."

Harry must have tugged the beard away from his face, because I heard him sticking up for me perfectly clearly. "No, no. The quiz was definitely Aunt Susan's idea."

Aunt Susan defended herself hotly. "No, it wasn't. Well, not that dreadful let's-have-the-questions-on-the-family-visit bit!"

That was too much for me. I stepped in, outraged. "That was Titania," I said. "That wasn't me."

Titania spread her hands and made her eyes go round as saucers. It was a really good Who—*me*? look, and I wished I'd seen it before I'd done my own performance a few minutes earlier.

Aunt Miriam's lip curled. "Look at the two of them," she said. "Acting all injured."

"If you put both of them in a bag and punched it, whichever one you hit would deserve it," said Great-granny.

"Excuse me," Mum told everyone. "I must just have a quick word with my son in private."

She led me outside again, while they kept grumbling about me. I could hear them through the door.

"Of course, you realize it was Ralph who sneaked to

everyone that I was having a few minutes' peace and quiet in the airing cupboard."

"*And* who gave poor little Titania that quite extraordinary letter purporting to be from the fairies at the bottom of the garden."

"And told everyone Great-aunt Ida's gifts had been around the block a good few times before ending up here."

"And made up all that rubbish about the brick."

Mum moved me further from the door. "Well?" she demanded. "Where are your aunt Miriam's earrings?"

"In your oyster-colored woolly tights," I said.

She looked a bit baffled. Then she looked appalled and rushed to the kitchen. Spread out all over the floor were great big slabs of oven and dozens of weirdly shaped metal bits. Grandpa broke off singing "Only Twenty-four Hours from Tulsa" to Bruno and said to Mum, "I'm pretty sure I'm winning here, Tansy, though there's a very strange pinging noise coming from somewhere . . ."

Mum spun round. Inside the washer, woollen things were tumbling over and over. We heard the pinging noise. We stepped closer. Then we heard it again. Louder.

Mum grabbed my arm and dragged me in front of the washing machine's little window. Among everything else swishing about, I could see a small clump of oyster-colored tights, and the pings seemed much louder.

"For heaven's sake!" wailed Mum. "I go through all the pockets! I shake out every fold! Who would have thought I'd have to start patting down my own hosiery?"

Just then, the washing machine switched onto Drain.

After a moment or two, the pinging suddenly seemed half as frequent. A moment after that, there was no pinging at all.

"Oh, no!" said Mum, horrified. "The pearls must have slipped through the drain holes."

Grandpa's eyes lit up. "We'll find them in the drain hose," he assured Mum. "All that I'll have to do is unscrew the facing, dismantle the lint trap and—"

Mum interrupted him. "You said all you had to do with the oven was take off the faulty catch. And now look at it!" She waved her hand over the junkyard spread across the floor.

So up to a point I have to say that I blame them. If those two hadn't been so busy scrapping about the mess Grandpa had made, one of them might have noticed that Aunt Miriam was creeping up behind us in the kitchen.

And, if they'd seen her, they might have warned me. Then I wouldn't have said it, and she wouldn't have heard:

"I doubt if you'll find them. They were horribly *small* pearls."

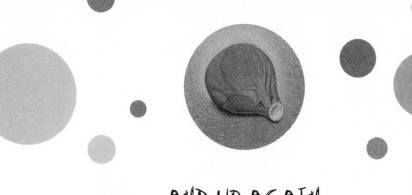

AND UP AGAIN

S o that's how I got sent upstairs again. Alone. On Christmas Day. With nothing to do but tell my side of the story.

Then Harry came up with supper on a tray. There was a heap of cold turkey and my favorite chutney, no Brussels sprouts at all, a pile of not "nicely browned" potatoes, and more sausages than I've ever been given at one time in my life.

"The extra sausages are from Dad," Harry told me, pulling a strand of beard out of my gravy and sucking it clean again. "There were even one or two more, but I ate them as a sort of tax for having to carry them up here."

"Good supper," I admitted. "They can't be all that mad at me."

"They're not mad at all. I think they're grateful, really. You've done them a giant favor."

"How?"

Harry stared. "Didn't you hear all that yelling and slamming and banging?"

"A bit of it," I admitted. "But I was busy writing something."

"You missed a royal battle," he informed me, pulling his beard down so I could hear him better. "First Aunt Miriam had the cheek to complain that your being sent upstairs wasn't enough of a punishment, given how careless you'd been with her pearls, and how rude you were about the size of them."

"Well, they *were* small."

"Exactly what Grandpa said. After he got round to taking out the spin drum, he made it clear to Bruno that, in his opinion, any pearl small enough to get through those drain holes was barely worth finding."

"Did Aunt Miriam hear him?"

"No, because Mum was coming on pretty strong at her that sending you upstairs was a perfectly adequate punishment, considering that Sylvia and Sylvester regularly damage our house, destroy our garden shed, tyrannize our pets and fling food over our garden, and they only get praise for it."

"Did Mum actually say that?"

Harry grinned. "She didn't just say it. She yelled it. And then there was a whole lot of door slamming and banging, and a good deal of talk about 'last straws.' And then Aunt Susan and Uncle Digby made the mistake of sticking up for Aunt Miriam by saying they hadn't felt terribly welcome either."

"I like that! They should try peeling whole mountains of potatoes and sleeping on a bed of lumps just so Titania doesn't have to look at tiny little stains on a wall!"

"More or less what Mum said. She certainly mentioned the potatoes. Then she went on for over half an hour about how ungrateful certain people were, even after certain other people had waited on them hand and foot for two full days."

He waggled the end of his beard at me.

"And by then, of course, you and poor Uncle Tristram had been rumbled about that fake letter from Santa. So Titania felt safe enough to come into the kitchen with her arms in the air, doing the spinny bits of her 'Welcome to My Fairy Wonderland' dance."

It was such a good story, I offered him another sausage.

"And of course she tripped over the neat little pile of stove burner rings Grandpa had laid out carefully on the floor."

"Chutney?"

He had a dip. "And went crashing into some other bits."

"Sharp bits?"

He looked ecstatic. "Sharp enough."

"I did hear screaming and wailing," I admitted. "I wasn't too busy to notice that. In fact, at one point I opened the door to try to find out what was happening."

"What did you hear?"

"Uncle Digby yelling that this house was a death trap."

"Did you hear Dad yelling back that it's a well-known fact that the best thing to do with a death trap is get out of it as fast as you can?"

"No," I said sadly. "I missed that. All I've heard since is footsteps pounding back and forth along the landing."

"That's them," said Harry. "Getting their stuff together."

"Are they leaving? All of them? Both lots?"

"Any minute. Mum says as soon as the coast is clear, you can come down again. But please to wait until you've heard both cars drive off, in case the sight of you sets them all off again and delays them."

"Righty-ho. I'll just stay here, tucking in, then."

He put his beard back on to go downstairs. At the door, he said something else.

"*What?*"

He pulled it away from his face for a moment. "And she says do you want cream or custard or ice cream with your Christmas pudding?"

"I'll have all three of them," I said.

(I think I know who's Mum's favorite today!)

SEASON'S GREETINGS

A HAPPY ENDING

By the time I came downstairs, the oven was intact again (except for a few stray pieces), but bits of the washing machine were still spread over the kitchen.

"While it's apart," Grandpa was explaining to Bruno, "it would be simply criminal not to give it a thorough servicing."

He went back to work and began to sing.

"Earl-ee one mo-or-ning,

Just as the sun was ri-i-sing . . ."

"Well, Grandpa's in good spirits," my dad told everyone. "Mind you, it's been a jubilee day for him. A whole oven torn to pieces. And now an entire washing machine in bits, for afters. Ralph's given Grandpa the best Christmas he could have imagined. He is perfectly happy."

"I'm happy too," said Uncle Tristram. "Nothing ever gives me more pleasure than seeing the back of Geoffrey."

Dad had to admit he had a few things to be grateful about as well. "The new shed is still standing. And, when you consider all that bread-roll throwing, I think the cat has borne up very well."

"And we'll be able to have risotto tomorrow without anyone *glowering*," Mum reminded him.

"I had a brilliant Christmas!" Harry admitted from behind his beard.

"And Albert learned a lot too," said Uncle Tristram.

"It's given Great-aunt Ida quite a lot to talk about when she goes back in her Home. If she remembers."

"*I* shall remember," said Great-granny. "I certainly shan't forget that excellent giving-people-half-a-brick trick."

"Don't bother wrapping one for me," my mum said cheerily. "This time next year I shall be lying on a beach in the Seychelles."

"Will we get presents if we have a beach holiday Christmas?" I asked my father.

"Certainly not," he said. "I can assure you that Santa will be pretty much bankrupt from the day he pays Holiday World the deposit."

"Pity," I said.

"Why?" he inquired. "Have you already drawn up a list of must-haves for next year?"

As it happens, he was being sarcastic. But up there in my room (Alone. On Christmas Day.) I had begun to draft the first rough version. No point in showing him, of course.

But so far, it looks like this:

RALPH'S CHRISTMAS LIST

A PAIR OF PLASTIC FANGS
A KUNG FU HAMSTER
A FART MACHINE
An ELECTRONIC VOICE CHANGER
A DESKTOP AIR CONDITIONER
A HUBERT the sheep WOOLLY SWEATER
A SECRET LAPEL BADGE CAMERA
A GIANT "CHASE 'em
& GET 'em" FLYCATCHER
A jet-BLACK BEANBAG with SILVER STRIPES
A REAL Bernese mountain DOG
A BOX OF PRINTED MAGGOT CHUTNEY LABELS
SWEET PEA SEEDS
A FLEA CIRCUS
A COLT ARMY REVOLVER
TWO BOXES OF FUDGE
BEDROOM KARAOKE
The COMPLETE WORKS OF Anne Fine
A SILVER COCKTAIL STIRRER (just LIKE GREAT-Aunt IDA'S)
A PAIR OF TRX24 PADDED hEADPHONES
A FURRY FAT hOT-WATER BOTTLE
An ELECTRIC POPCORN MAKER
TWO INFLATABLE SLEEPING BAGS
A SILVER hip FLASK
A STUFFED SKUNK
LICORICE BOOTLACES (BLACK, not RED)
A BOX OF just-FILL-in-the-BLANKS, PREPRINTED thANK-YOU LETTERS

ABOUT THE AUTHOR

ANNE FINE is the Children's Laureate of Great Britain and a two-time winner of England's highest literary award, the Carnegie Medal. She has written many highly acclaimed books for young readers, including *Up on Cloud Nine*, which *School Library Journal* praised in a starred review as "a gift to those who know and love others who are different." She is also the author of *Alias Madame Doubtfire*, on which the Robin Williams movie hit *Mrs. Doubtfire* was based; *Flour Babies; The Tulip Touch*; and *Bad Dreams*. The mother of two daughters, Anne Fine lives in County Durham, England.